THE SCIENCE OF SPEED

THE SCIENCE OF CAR RACING

by Karen Latchana Kenney

CONSULTANT:
PAUL OHMANN, PH.D
ASSOCIATE PROFESSOR AND CHAIR OF PHYSICS
UNIVERSITY OF ST. THOMAS, MINNESOTA

CAPSTONE PRESS
a capstone imprint

Velocity is published by Capstone Press,
1710 Roe Crest Drive, North Mankato, Minnesota 56003.
www.capstonepub.com

Copyright © 2014 by Capstone Press, a Capstone imprint.
All rights reserved. No part of this publication may be reproduced in whole or in part, or stored in a retrieval system, or transmitted in any form or by any means, electronic, mechanical, photocopying, recording, or otherwise, without written permission of the publisher.
For information regarding permission, write to Capstone Press,
1710 Roe Crest Drive, North Mankato, Minnesota 56003.

Library of Congress Cataloging-in-Publication Data
Kenney, Karen Latchana, author.
  The science of car racing / by Karen Latchana Kenney.
      pages cm.—(Velocity—the science of speed)
  Summary: "Describes the science concepts involved in several types of car racing"—Provided by publisher.
  Audience: Ages 10–14.
  Audience: Grades 4 to 6.
  ISBN 978-1-4765-3910-2 (library binding)
  ISBN 978-1-4765-5193-7 (pbk.)
  ISBN 978-1-4765-6058-8 (ebook PDF)
  1. Automobile racing—Juvenile literature. 2. Automobiles, Racing—Design and construction—Juvenile literature. I. Title. II. Series: Velocity (Capstone Press)
  GV1029.13.K46 2014
  796.72—dc23   2013026811

Editorial Credits
Adrian Vigliano, editor; Kyle Grenz, designer; Laura Manthe, production specialist

Photo Credits
Dreamstime: Lawrence Weslowski Jr, 21, Walter Arce, cover, Zepherwind, 16-17; Getty Images for NASCAR: Jason Smith, 11 (top), Todd Warshaw, 27 (top); Getty Images: AFP/Josep Lago, 18-19 (top), AFP/Tom Gandolfini, 30-31, Archive Photos/Robert Alexander, 29 (inset), Bill Pugliano, 14-15, Patrick Smith, 34, Tom Pennington, 44-45; Newscom/Cal Sport Media/Walter G Arce, 28-29, Icon SMI/Brain Cleary, 23, Icon SMI/Kyle Ocker, 12-13, Icon SMI/Marc Sanchez, 33, Octane Photographic Ltd/Leanne Wilson, 43; Shutterstock: 333DIGIT, 10 (top), Action Sports Photography, 4-5, 6, 10-11, 24-25, 26, 27 (bottom), 32, 36-37 (bottom), 42, Beelde Photography, 8 (top), 13 (top), 36-37 (top), 40-41, David Huntley Creative, 35, EvrenKalinbacak, 38, 39, fotographic1980, (background, throughout), Max Earey, 45 (inset), Mikhail Kolesnikov, 9, Natursports, 8 (bottom), Phillip Rubino, 16 (left), Sandra R. Barba, 20, Studio 1a Photography, 18-19 (bottom)

Printed in the United States of America in Stevens Point, Wisconsin.
092013   007767WZS14

TABLE OF CONTENTS

INTRODUCTION: 4
CAR RACING SCIENCE 4

CHAPTER 1:
START YOUR ENGINES! 6
CONVERTING ENERGY 6
AIR IN, AIR OUT 8
BIG POWER 10
FIGHTING ENGINE FRICTION 12

CHAPTER 2:
RACE CAR DESIGN 14
THE POWER OF AIR 14
PUTTING AIR TO WORK 16
UNDER PRESSURE 18
USING TRACTION 20
COMING TO A STOP 22

CHAPTER 3:
IN THE DRIVER'S SEAT 24
A DRIVER'S BODY 24
HIGH-SPEED CRASHES 26
SAFE HEADGEAR 28
FIREPROOF SUITS 30

CHAPTER 4:
ON THE TRACK 32
FAST CARS 32
TURNING FORCES 34
HIGH-SPEED DRAFTING 36
RALLY JUMPS 38
FINDING BALANCE 40

CHAPTER 5:
TRACK DESIGN 42
RACE TRACK ENGINEERS 42
FULL SPEED AHEAD 44

BACK MATTER 46
GLOSSARY 46
READ MORE 47
INTERNET SITES 47
INDEX 48

Introduction:
Car Racing Science

It's a constant battle on the racetrack. Weight, heat, and **air resistance** are just a few things that slow down race cars. Engines work hard so cars can reach top speeds.

Combustion: Inside the engine, the combustion of fuel in air creates the car's power.

Friction: There is friction between the tires and the track. The high amount of friction allows cars to grip the road at high speeds.

air resistance—the force the air puts on an object moving through it
combustion—the process of catching on fire and then burning
friction—a rubbing motion between one surface and another

Science is involved with almost everything in car racing. Physics and forces affect how wheels grip the track, the car's speed, and how the car moves. Chemistry is at work creating the power in the engine. And biology is important too. A driver's body goes through a lot of stress in a race. Scientific knowledge helps racers understand what they need to do to cross the finish line first.

Downforce: A rear wing controls the downforce of air as it flows over the car, keeping the tires stuck to the track.

downforce—a force that acts on a moving vehicle to push it down toward the ground

Chapter 1:
Start Your Engines!

CONVERTING ENERGY

Car racing is all about motion. That motion starts in the engine. Fuel contains the energy that is **converted** into a car's motion. The energy is locked inside the fuel's **molecules** as chemical energy. To release the energy, a **chemical reaction** occurs. In an engine's combustion chamber, fuel is mixed with air and then ignited. The result is carbon dioxide, water, and a whole lot of motion energy.

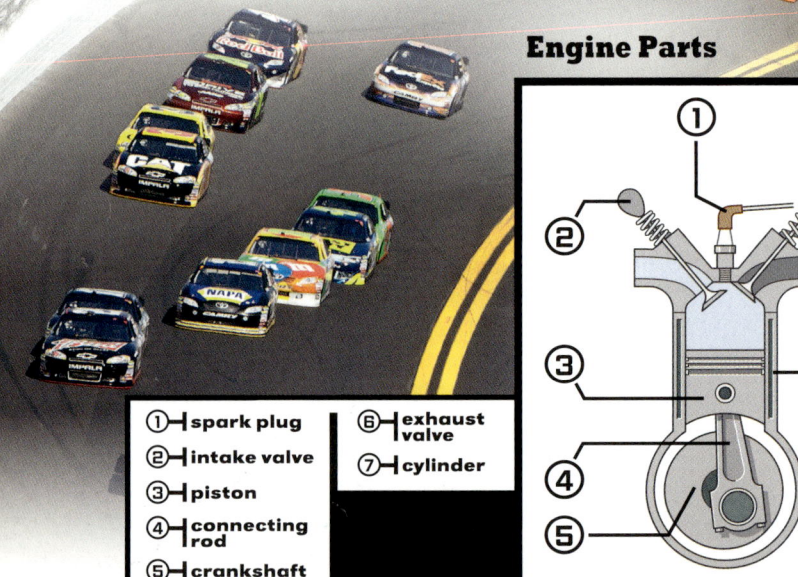

Engine Parts

① spark plug
② intake valve
③ piston
④ connecting rod
⑤ crankshaft
⑥ exhaust valve
⑦ cylinder

convert—when something, such as energy, changes form
molecule—a group of atoms connected by a bond; an atom is the smallest form of an element
chemical reaction—process in which one or more substances are made into a new substance or substances

There are four strokes in the cycle of an engine. One of those strokes is compression. This is when the fuel and air in the combustion chamber are pushed into a smaller space. This stroke gets the mixture ready to be ignited. This ignition starts the chemical reaction inside an engine.

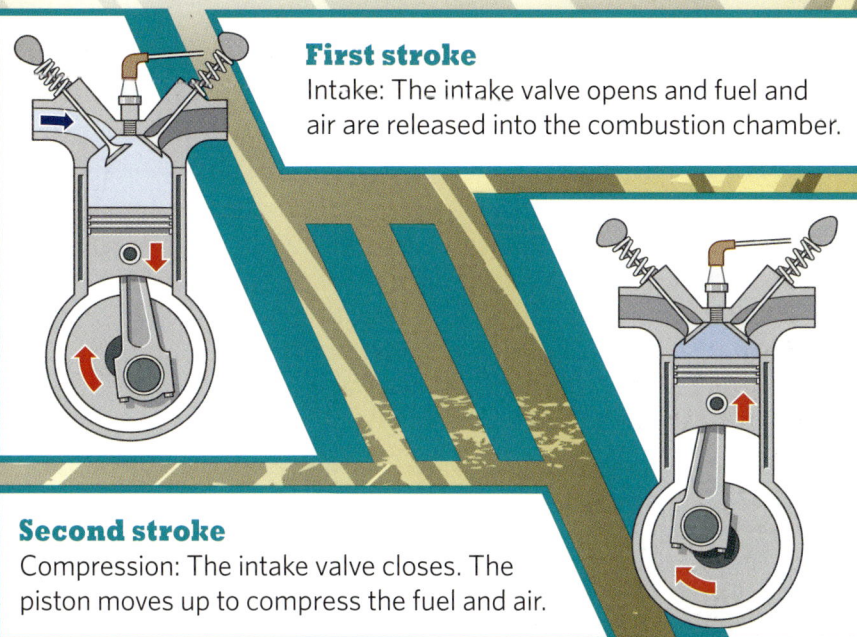

First stroke
Intake: The intake valve opens and fuel and air are released into the combustion chamber.

Second stroke
Compression: The intake valve closes. The piston moves up to compress the fuel and air.

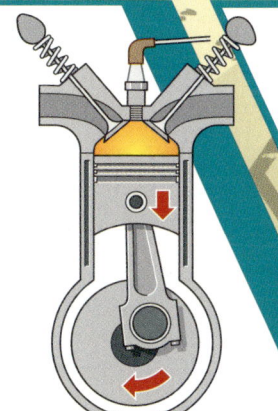

Third stroke
Power: A spark plug creates a spark and ignites the mixture. Energy is released from the fuel and air. The energy forces the piston down, moving other parts in the engine.

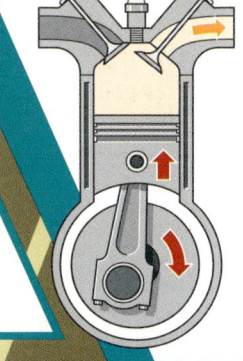

Fourth stroke
Exhaust: The piston moves up again and the exhaust valve opens. Gases are pushed out of the combustion chamber.

AIR IN, AIR OUT

Bigger explosions in the combustion chamber make a race car travel even faster. One way to add more power is to get as much cool air into the engine as possible. Cool air has more densely packed molecules than hot air. That means there is more oxygen to burn. Formula 1 (F1) cars use an air box to let more air into the engine. The air box catches outside air as the car moves and feeds it to the engine.

cold air box
The air box allows more cool air to get to an engine.

FACT
The sound level on some race cars can be as high as 105 decibels (dB). That is 32,000 times louder than a normal conversation!

It is also important for an engine to breathe. As more air comes in, more needs to get out. This is where the exhaust system comes in. Race car exhaust systems are designed to let gases exit quickly.

The loud roar of a race car is hard to ignore. Part of that sound comes from the exhaust. Most race cars don't have mufflers, which is the part that makes regular passenger cars quieter. That's because mufflers slow down cars by creating **pressure** on the engine. Without a muffler, the full sound of an engine escapes in waves. This makes air molecules move and bounce against one another. When the sound hits the fans' ears, it is really loud!

pressure—the force made by pressing on something

BIG POWER

An engine itself doesn't really create power, though. It just transfers energy from the fuel to the wheels. Energy cannot be created or destroyed. It just moves from one form to another. This is called energy transfer. And in a race car, there is a lot of energy that is transferred. A NASCAR engine has about 850 **horsepower** (hp). An average car only has about 228 hp!

The Power of Horses

James Watt invented the term horsepower in the late 1700s. Steam engines had just been invented and Watt needed a term to explain their power. He examined the jobs steam engines could do. Then he compared each job with the number of horses it would take to do the same thing. The number of horses the engine was replacing was the horsepower of the engine.

The power of a car is defined as how fast an engine transfers the energy from fuel into motion. NASCAR racers use their superpowered engines to reach speeds of more than 200 miles (322 km) per hour.

horsepower—a unit for measuring an engine's power

FIGHTING ENGINE FRICTION

High speed and big power mean that a race car engine works really hard. Its parts move over and over, rubbing against each other in the process. This creates heat and friction, which slows down an engine. Friction isn't always bad. It is what makes a race car's brakes work. But it is never a good thing in a race car's engine. The result can cause overheating—a serious problem.

Oil is the key to fighting friction. This liquid seals in the gases and lets the parts glide smoothly against one another. This smoothness allows the engine to move quickly, but with less heat involved.

Engine oil comes in different "weights." These weights affect how hard an engine works. A lower-weight oil can help the car get a little more horsepower on shorter runs. But higher-weight oils can stand up to harder-working engines during full races. Race car teams use different oil weights for different kinds of races. For NASCAR qualifying races, zero-weight oil might be used. But for other races, crews might choose 10- to 30-weight oils.

Chapter 2:
Race Car Design

THE POWER OF AIR

Air resistance can be a real drag. It can slow down a car. Air flows under and over a race car. Billions of air molecules also push against it during a race, causing air resistance. **Aerodynamics** is the study of this airflow. Understanding how to adjust it can give drivers an edge on the track.

aerodynamics—the study of airflow to reduce air resistance

Engineers design a race car to let air flow smoothly over the body. When the body is shaped with aerodynamics in mind, less of its surface hits air molecules. To understand airflow, some cars are tested in a wind tunnel. In F1 racing, even drivers' helmets are part of the tests.

A wind tunnel is a hollow tube-shaped room. At one end are very powerful fans. These fans make a flow of air through the tunnel and over the car. Special sensors measure how the air interacts with the car. Scientists study the data to understand the **lift** and drag on the car. This information is critical for car designers. They make changes to the car, helping it gain speed and have more downforce.

lift—the upward force on a vehicle

PUTTING AIR TO WORK

Car designers have two big goals—reduce drag and increase downforce. If they can reduce drag, they can increase speed. With more downforce, the cars can grip the track better at high speeds.

Race cars are designed to let air flow smoothly over the body. Unlike passenger cars, the side mirrors on NASCAR cars do not stick out from the body. Front grilles are partially taped over so air cannot enter the engine there. The tape directs air over the top surface of the car, creating a smoother flow. The front of the cars sit low to the ground, almost touching the track. Keeping the car low directs as much air as possible over the top surface of the car.

A few things can help increase downforce:

Wings extend above the rear of many race cars, such as stock cars and Indy cars. Some race cars also have a front wing. The flat part of a wing adjusts to different angles. Low angles produce less drag but also less downforce. High angles create more drag but also more downforce. Crews adjust the wings to fit what the cars need for the track.

wing

Splitters are flat pieces that extend out parallel to the ground from the front of some race cars. They split the air. Lower pressure air goes below the car. High-pressure air goes above the car. A splitter allows more force to push down on the car. Cars in NASCAR and Formula 1 use splitters.

splitter

UNDER PRESSURE

Tires are under a lot of stress during a race. They wear down quickly, and pressure grows inside the tires. The increasing pressure can lead to a tire blowout, which can end the race.

Gases inflate tires. Most normal cars use regular air inside tires. But many race cars use pure nitrogen instead. As a race car goes faster, the friction between the tires and the road increases. This creates a lot of heat. As the tires heat up, the gas inside the tires heats up. All of this heat makes the gas molecules move around more. As they move, they need to take up more space. The molecules push against the sides of the tires more, increasing the pressure.

In air there is nitrogen but also a small amount of water. These water molecules can really increase the pressure. But in pure nitrogen, there are no water molecules. Nitrogen makes smaller changes in tire pressure, making it better for use in racing.

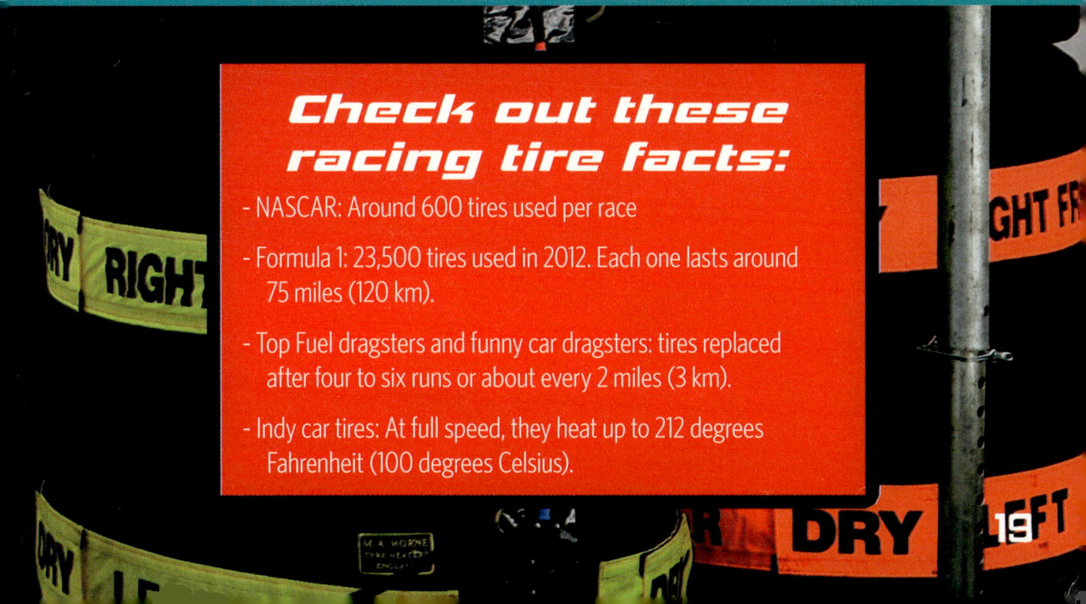

Check out these racing tire facts:

- NASCAR: Around 600 tires used per race

- Formula 1: 23,500 tires used in 2012. Each one lasts around 75 miles (120 km).

- Top Fuel dragsters and funny car dragsters: tires replaced after four to six runs or about every 2 miles (3 km).

- Indy car tires: At full speed, they heat up to 212 degrees Fahrenheit (100 degrees Celsius).

USING TRACTION

Traction is good in racing. It keeps race cars on the track. It also helps racers with **acceleration**, turning, and stopping. Traction is the frictional force between the tires and the track. Unlike engine friction, tire friction is something racers want.

Two things control how much traction a race car has: how well the tires stick to the track and the amount of force pushing down on the tires. Downforce is really important for traction. The car's weight also pushes down on the tires.

Formula 1 cars use different tire treads depending on the conditions of the track.

acceleration—the rate of change of speed

Most race cars use tires without treads called racing slicks. Treads are made to channel water away from tires on wet days. Without treads, more of a tire's surface touches the track. With more contact, the tires create more friction. This makes for better traction. These tires can't be used in the rain, though. That's why NASCAR cars do not race in the rain. Formula 1 and a few other types of race cars use special treaded rain tires.

COMING TO A STOP

Friction is important for something else—braking. The brakes are hardworking parts on a race car. They have to stop or slow cars traveling at incredible speeds. Brakes create huge amounts of heat and wear down quickly.

Disc Brake Parts

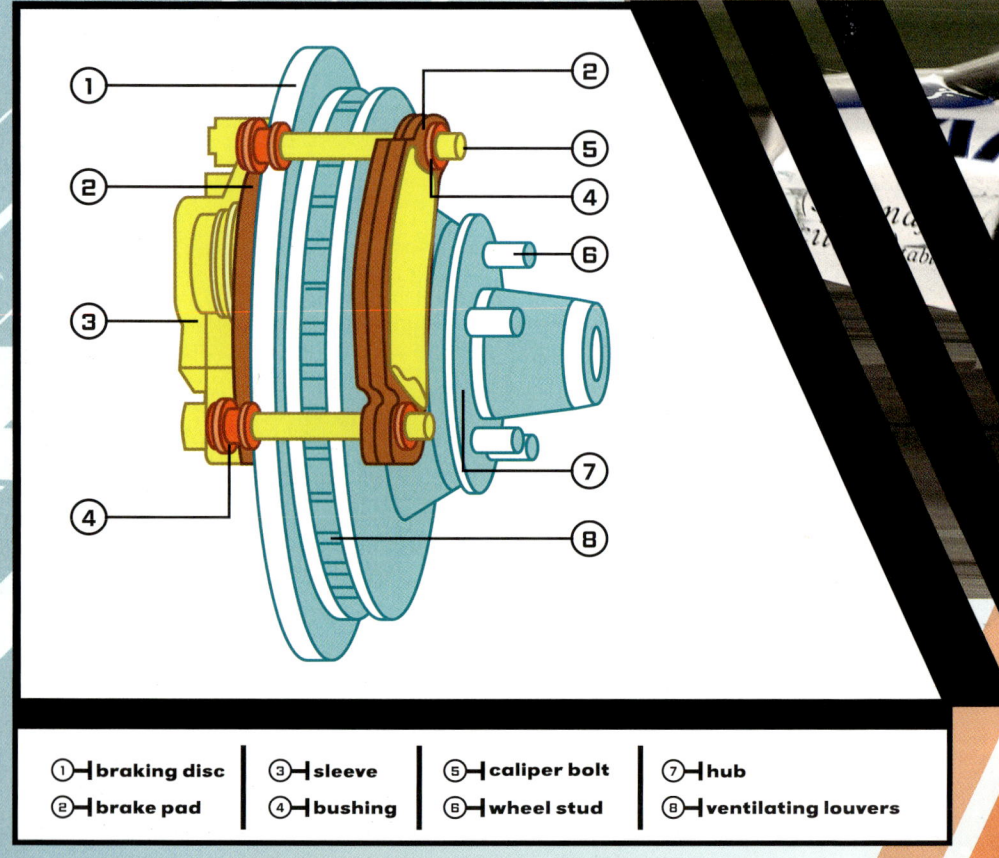

1. braking disc
2. brake pad
3. sleeve
4. bushing
5. caliper bolt
6. wheel stud
7. hub
8. ventilating louvers

FACT
Race car brake discs are made of carbon fiber. This tough material doesn't melt from the high temperatures produced during a race.

Here's how car brakes work. The brake pads push against the brake rotor. The brake rotor is a disc connected to the wheel. As the brake pads push, they create friction, which slows down the car. But the friction also makes the brake pad and rotor heat up. This temperature can go higher than 1,832°F (1,000°C) in Formula 1 cars. Stock car brake pads work best around 1,100°F (593°C), but can get much hotter.

The brake rotors on a stock car glow bright red from the heat.

If brake pads get too hot, they stop making as much friction. For stock car racers this can be a big problem. They make several turns on each lap, braking for long periods of time. Sometimes the brakes glow red because of the heat they make. Crews put a special paint on the brake rotors. The paint **oxidizes** when it reaches a certain temperature. By looking at the brake rotors, crews know how hot the rotors got during a certain race.

oxidize—to combine chemically with oxygen, which can make a substance look different in color or texture

Chapter 3:
In the Driver's Seat

A DRIVER'S BODY

Drivers are real athletes during an intense race. Here's what a driver is up against:

HEART RATE Heart rate can speed up to 120 to 150 beats per minute. Some drivers reach the same heart rates as Olympic long distance swimmers and marathon runners.

MUSCLE STRENGTH Some drivers are pulled sideways with the same force astronauts feel during takeoff. Drivers need strong abdominal muscles to stay upright. The brake pedal can feel like it weighs 300 pounds (136 kg) when drivers push it down. Drivers need to have strong quad muscles. Their hands have to be really strong too. Some drivers grip the wheel for several hours.

HIGH-SPEED CRASHES

Crashes are bound to happen. And when they do, watch out! A whole lot of energy will be released. When cars are speeding on the track, they have **kinetic energy**. This is the energy of motion. When that motion stops in a crash, the energy has to go somewhere. It can't disappear, since energy cannot be destroyed.

At impact, a car's kinetic energy disperses. This energy dispersal may crush or snap parts of the car or cause damage to the track.

Race cars are built to absorb some crash energy by crumpling in certain areas. NASCAR cars crumple at the front and rear. Metal is thrown off the body, taking away more energy from the car.

kinetic energy—the energy of movement

SAFER Barriers

The Steel and Foam Energy Reduction (SAFER) barrier is a special wall installed on the edges of many tracks. SAFER barriers use a mixture of foam and steel tubes to absorb and reduce the kinetic energy of a race car accident. If a car hits the track's SAFER barrier, the barrier absorbs 30 to 50 percent of the energy. The energy crushes the barrier on impact.

As the brakes are used and the car skids, more energy is released as heat. And have you heard a crash's loud sound? That is more of the kinetic energy being released.

SAFE HEADGEAR

When a crash happens, the car stops quickly. But the driver is still moving forward. This is called **inertia**—a mass that is moving tends to keep moving in the same direction. But car safety features slow that forward motion.

A head injury can kill a driver instantly. If a driver's head bends too far forward, it can cause the skull to crack. A safety harness keeps the driver's torso and pelvis in place. But the head can easily snap forward. That's why the Head and Neck Support (HANS) device is so important in NASCAR races. It is a collar that attaches to the driver's helmet and harness. It keeps the head from moving separately from the body.

inertia—an object's state in which the object stays at rest or keeps moving in the same direction until a force acts on the object

The helmet also absorbs energy. If the driver's head crashes into something, the helmet's interior crushes and absorbs some of the impact energy. The energy spreads throughout the material of the helmet. The crushing spreads the force out over a longer time.

Dale Earnhardt Sr.

Dale Earnhardt Sr. was once one of the best NASCAR drivers. But on February 18, 2001, he had a fatal crash during the Daytona 500. He was not wearing a HANS device (most drivers did not use the HANS device at that time). He died from trauma to his head. After Earnhardt's tragic death, using the HANS device was required for NASCAR drivers.

FIREPROOF SUITS

Leaked fuel from a crash can ignite into a powerful blaze. So it's important to protect drivers' bodies as well as their heads. Fire suits have this vital job.

Gasoline fires can reach between 1,200 and 1,800°F (649 and 982°C). Everyday clothing fabrics such as cotton, polyester, and rayon catch fire between 250 and 540°F (121 and 282°C).

Fire suits are made from a special fabric. It resists catching fire up to a point. It buys drivers a bit of time to escape the wreck or wait until the fire is put out. The fabric in NASCAR suits does not melt or burn. Instead it starts to char when heated up to high temperatures. Drivers also wear fire-resistant underwear, gloves, and boots.

FACT
NASCAR requires that suits protect drivers from a fire burning at 1,800°F (982°C) for five seconds.

F1 Safety

F1 suits have another special feature. On each shoulder is a large handle. The car seat in an F1 car can be easily released in case of a crash. The driver can then be quickly pulled out of the car while still strapped into the seat. The suit's handles are strong enough to support the weight of the driver and the seat.

Chapter 4:
On the Track

FAST CARS

Race cars reach high speeds during a race. Speed is the measure of how far an object can go in a certain amount of time. But to get to that speed, the car needs to accelerate. It starts at rest, with a speed of 0 miles per hour. Then it changes speed to start the race.

Forces are what make acceleration possible. Sir Isaac Newton was a great scientist and mathematician born in the 1600s. He came up with three laws about motion. His second law states that an unbalanced force acts upon an object to cause acceleration. It can cause an object to stop as well.

For race cars, the engine produces large forces. These forces are transferred to push the car forward, making it accelerate. The forces are greater than those pushing the car back. So the car accelerates forward because unbalanced forces act upon it.

Check out the fast acceleration rates found in car racing:

Car	Acceleration
Formula 1	0–100 miles (0–161 km) per hour in 3.5 seconds
Top Fuel Dragster	0–100 miles (0–161 km) per hour in less than 0.8 seconds
Indy Car	0–100 miles (0–161 km) per hour in less than 3 seconds
Rally Car	0–62 miles (0–100 km) per hour in about 3 seconds

FACT

Drag race cars have to accelerate as quickly as possible because the tracks they race on are so short. Some dragsters can accelerate to more than 300 miles (483 km) per hour in less than 5 seconds.

TURNING FORCES

Going straight is pretty simple, but turns are tricky. With oval tracks, there are four turns on each lap. That means race cars spend a lot of their time turning. Speed and momentum can be lost during those tricky turns.

Centripetal force is what makes race cars turn. This force keeps an object moving in a curved path. It pulls the race car toward the center of the track. Friction between the tires and the track makes this force, which is measured in g. One g equals the force of Earth's **gravity**.

centripetal force—the force that pulls an object turning in a circle inward toward the center
gravity—a force that pulls objects toward the center of Earth

During turns, NASCAR drivers feel a force of 2 to 3 gs. Indy Car and Formula 1 drivers feel forces of 4 to 5 gs.

Have you seen how NASCAR tracks tilt up at the turns? This is called banking. It helps the cars turn at faster speeds. On the tilted turns, the car is pushed toward the center of the track. This adds to the centripetal force on the car.

centripetal force

bank angle

FACT
NASCAR tracks bank at different degrees. Talladega Superspeedway has the steepest bank at 33 degrees. New Hampshire Motor Speedway's bank is just 7 degrees.

HIGH-SPEED DRAFTING

Two cars speed just inches from each other in a NASCAR race. Why are they driving so close? They're drafting. It's a driving technique that uses aerodynamics to increase speed.

The front of the car cuts and displaces air.

Low pressure creates drag. Greater downforce results in greater drag.

When cars are far apart, they each have to punch through a wall of air. The air makes a low-pressure area behind each car. This slows down the cars.

When drafting, one car tucks in inches behind another car. It sits in the car's low-pressure area. The air then flows over both cars as if they were one car. The car in front is then pushing the air molecules for both cars. This reduces drag on both cars.

36

Junior Johnson

The first driver to use drafting in a NASCAR race was Junior Johnson. He won the Daytona 500 in 1960 by drafting. He was driving a much slower car than the other racers. But with drafting Johnson was in the lead for 67 of the 200 laps. He went on to win the race. It was his first win of the season. Ever since, drafting has been key to winning NASCAR races.

The first car can go faster. And the second car gets pulled along with the first. Together, the cars can go 5 miles (8 km) per hour faster than they can on their own.

Rear car fills the low-pressure area, reducing drag on the front car.

RALLY JUMPS

Jumps are a big part of rally racing. Rally cars completely lift off the ground. They fly through the air. Then somehow they land in one piece back on the ground.

Speed keeps the car moving forward while in the air. But too much speed can be a bad thing. As rally driver Jari-Matti Latvala explains, it is best to reduce speed before jumping. If the car has too much speed, the air will produce a downforce that pushes the rear of the car down. But some acceleration while jumping creates a smoother landing by keeping the wheels moving. Rally drivers must learn to jump and land well without losing too much speed.

Landing has a lot of impact on the car. To absorb that energy, rally cars have special shock-absorbing suspensions that can handle extra impact. Rally cars also use dampers to absorb impact energy. Dampers are filled with oil. The oil absorbs heat energy, creating smoother landings. There are four dampers on a pro rally car.

Off-Road Hill Climbing

Hill-climb racing is one of the oldest forms of car racing. In off-road hill climbing races, the goal is to get to the top of a steep hill in the shortest amount of time possible. The distances are usually short, but these races go up mountains on narrow and winding roads. This type of racing is a true fight against gravity.

FINDING BALANCE

Sometimes drivers get all the glory. But racing is truly a team sport. Without a race crew, the driver would not be nearly as good on the track.

In the **pit**, it's a fast race to find a car's balance. Balance is critical to winning the race. It's when both ends of the car grip the track equally. Drivers know right away when the balance is off.

pit—the area where cars stop for service during a race

Tires gain pressure during a race, making them wear down quickly. This affects how well they can grip the track. And as fuel burns, the car gets lighter. This changes the **center of gravity** of the car. Balance problems can begin to change the way the car handles. These problems can stop a driver from winning.

Pit crews change tires and fuel cars within seconds during a race. It's their job to find and keep a car as balanced as possible during a race.

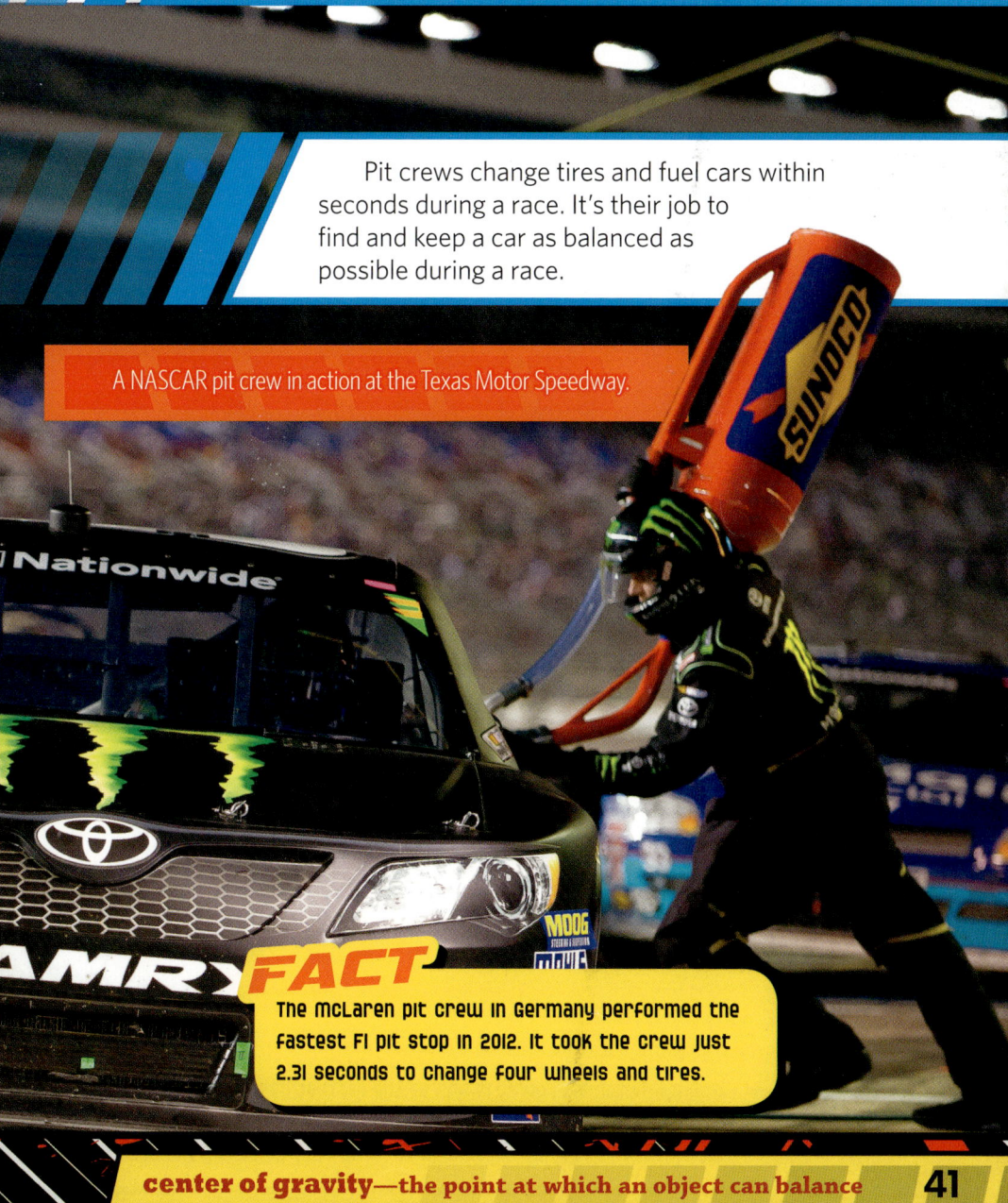

A NASCAR pit crew in action at the Texas Motor Speedway.

FACT

The McLaren pit crew in Germany performed the fastest F1 pit stop in 2012. It took the crew just 2.31 seconds to change four wheels and tires.

center of gravity—the point at which an object can balance

Chapter 5:
Track Design

RACE TRACK ENGINEERS

Race tracks have different shapes and angles. Some have more turns than others. And their banking angles can vary quite a bit. It takes a lot of planning to design a race track.

Engineers design race tracks. They have to follow the rules set out by the governing group for each type of racing. Formula 1 allows banking angles to go up by only 10 percent on curves. NASCAR requires the SAFER barriers on its track. Engineers also think about the space they have to work with. They must balance the rules set out with designing a challenging track.

FACT

Atlanta Motor Speedway is one of the fastest NASCAR tracks. It is a quad-oval track that is 1.54 miles (2.48 km) long. It banks at 24 degrees. Its racing surface is 55 to 60 feet (17 to 18 m) wide.

There are also different shapes and types to consider. NASCAR has four track types: short, intermediate, superspeedway, and road course. Most NASCAR tracks are oval, but there are different oval shapes. Tri-oval and D-shaped oval tracks have five turns instead of four.

Corners and Tracks

Drivers take corners seriously. They can quickly destroy a lead or make a race. Here are two of the most challenging corners on F1 tracks.

- Monza Parabolica: This final turn in the track stretches 180 degrees. Cars can get up to 124 miles (200 km) per hour going around the turn.
- Istanbul Park's Turn Eight: Drivers reach speeds of 168 miles (270 km) per hour going around this intense corner.

oval

tri-oval

D-Shaped oval

quad-oval

43

FULL SPEED AHEAD

Car racing is thrilling to watch. Up in the stands, fans see the high speeds cars reach and hear the loud roar of the engines. On the track crews work to tweak car engines and keep cars performing at their best. And behind the wheel, drivers' bodies and minds work hard to control these powerful machines.

24 Hours of Le Mans

The 24 Hours of Le Mans is an endurance race that takes place every year in France. Teams of three drivers race for 24 hours. The race is a big challenge for everyone on a team. Drivers must share driving time to stay rested and alert. Crews have to keep the car balanced and running smoothly for the entire race. Cars race more than 3,100 miles (4,989 km) during Le Mans.

Science is a huge part of car racing—from the physics on the track to the biology of the racer. It takes skill and knowledge to make cars race at top speeds. And crews and drivers know how to make science work on their side.

Back-Matter
GLOSSARY

acceleration (ak-sel-uh-RAY-shuhn)—the rate of change of speed

aerodynamics (ayr-oh-dy-NA-miks)—the study of airflow to reduce air resistance

air resistance (AIR ri-ZISS-tuhnss)—the force the air puts on an object moving through it

center of gravity (SEN-tur UHV GRAV-uh-tee)—the point at which an object can balance

centripetal force (sen-TRI-puh-tuhl FORSS)—the force that pulls an object turning in a circle inward toward the center

chemical reaction (KE-muh-kuhl ree-AK-shuhn)—process in which one or more substances are made into a new substance or substances

combustion (kuhm-BUS-chuhn)—the process of catching on fire and then burning

convert (kuhn-VURT)—when something, such as energy, changes form

downforce (DOUN-forss)—a force that acts on a moving vehicle that pushes it down toward the ground

friction (FRIK-shuhn)—a rubbing motion between one surface and another

gravity (GRAV-uh-tee)—a force that pulls objects toward the center of Earth

horsepower (HORSS-pou-ur)—a unit for measuring an engine's power

inertia (in-UR-shuh)—an object's state in which the object stays at rest or keeps moving in the same direction until a force acts on the object

kinetic energy (ki-NET-ik EN-ur-jee)—the energy of movement

lift (LIFT)—the upward force on a vehicle

molecule (MOL-uh-kyool)—a group of atoms connected by a bond; an atom is the smallest form of an element

oxidize (OK-suh-dyze)—to combine chemically with oxygen, which can make a substance look different in color or texture

pit (PIT)—the area where cars stop for service during a race

pressure (PRESH-ur)—the force made by pressing on something

READ MORE

Hammond, Richard. *Car Science.* New York: DK Publishing, 2008.

Howard, Melanie A. *Stock Cars.* North Mankato, Minn.: Capstone Press, 2011.

Murray, Robb. *A Daredevil's Guide to Car Racing.* North Mankato, Minn.: Capstone Press, 2013.

Schwartz, Heather E. *The Science of a Race Car: Reactions in Action.* North Mankato, Minn.: Capstone Press, 2010.

INTERNET SITES

FactHound offers a safe, fun way to find Internet sites related to this book. All of the sites on FactHound have been researched by our staff.

Here's all you do:

Visit *www.facthound.com*

Enter this code: 9781476539102

INDEX

balance, 40, 41, 45

braking, 12, 22, 23, 24, 27

crashes, 26, 27, 28, 29, 30

drafting, 36, 37

dragsters, 19, 33

Earnhardt, Dale (Sr.), 29

Formula 1 (F1), 8, 15, 17, 19, 20, 21, 23, 31, 33, 35, 41, 42, 43

fuel, 4, 6, 7, 10, 11, 30, 41

gravity, 34, 39, 41

Head and Neck Support (HANS) device, 28–29

heart rates, 24

helmets, 15, 28, 29

hill-climb racing, 39

Indy Car, 17, 19, 33, 35

injuries, 28, 29

Johnson, Junior, 37

jumps, 38

NASCAR, 10, 11, 13, 16, 17, 19, 21, 26, 28, 29, 30, 31, 35, 36, 37, 40, 41, 42, 43

pit crews, 40, 41

rally cars, 33, 38, 39

Steel and Foam Energy Reduction (SAFER) barriers, 27, 42

shock absorbers, 39

suspensions, 39

Top Fuel, 19, 33

tracks, 4, 5, 14, 16, 17, 20, 21, 26, 27, 33, 34, 35, 40, 41, 42, 43, 44, 45

wind tunnels, 15